YOU MAY JUST BE A DINOSAUR

WRITTEN BY
HEATHER MACHT

ILLUSTRATED BY
JASON GILLARD

PELICAN PUBLISHNG COMPANY
Gretna 2015

The word "Pelican" and the depiction of a pelican are trademarks of Pelican Publishing Company, Inc., and are registered in the U.S. Patent and Trademark Office.

Library of Congress Cataloging-in-Publication Data

Macht, Heather.
  You may just be a dinosaur / by Heather Macht ; illustrated by Jason Gillard.
     pages cm
  Summary: "Is your toothbrush too small, and do you look for leaves for breakfast instead of cereal? You may just be a dinosaur! Find out in this rhyming picture book for young readers. Educational facts about the stegosaurus, tyrannosaurus rex, and other dinosaurs are included"-- Provided by publisher.
  Includes bibliographical references.
  ISBN 978-1-4556-2040-1 (hardcover : alk. paper) -- ISBN 978-1-4556-2041-8 (e-book) [1. Stories in rhyme. 2. Dinosaurs--Fiction.] I. Gillard, Jason, illustrator. II. Title.
  PZ8.3.M13155Yo 2015
  [E]--dc23
                                    2014028325

Printed in Malaysia
Published by Pelican Publishing Company, Inc.
1000 Burmaster Street, Gretna, Louisiana 70053

To Hunter OZ Macht, Mommy's little T. rex —H. M.

For my ladybirds —J. G.

When you wake every morning,
what's the first thing you do?

Do you look for cereal to eat or for leaves to chew?

Can't brush your teeth because your toothbrush is too small? Do you wish you had one made for someone really tall?

If this sounds like you, then I'm pretty sure you may just be a dinosaur!

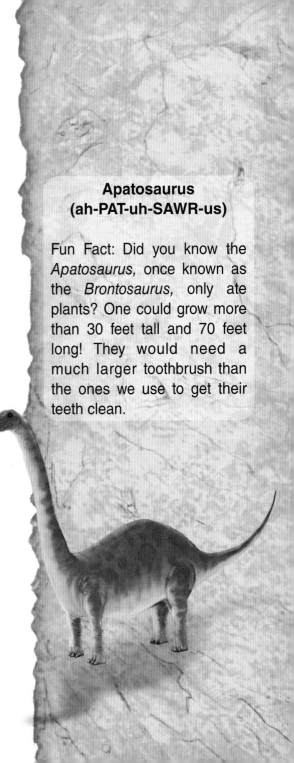

Apatosaurus
(ah-PAT-uh-SAWR-us)

Fun Fact: Did you know the *Apatosaurus*, once known as the *Brontosaurus*, only ate plants? One could grow more than 30 feet tall and 70 feet long! They would need a much larger toothbrush than the ones we use to get their teeth clean.

Do none of the clothes in your closet fit? Do the plates down your back make your shirt and pants split?

Is something missing when you try to brush your hair? When you look in the mirror, do you notice nothing's there?

If you answered yes to one question or more, then you may just be a dinosaur!

**Stegosaurus
(STEG-uh-SAWR-us)**

Fun Fact: *Stegosaurus* had 17 bony plates that went down its back and tail. It also had large spikes at the end of its tail. Do you think the plates and spikes would rip a *Stegosaurus's* clothing?

When you try to take the school bus and can't fit inside, does everyone hop on your back for a ride?

When you try to speak, do you actually roar?

Do you have a long, scaly tail, but you're not sure what for? Then you may just be a dinosaur!

**Tyrannosaurus
(tye-RAN-uh-SAWR-us)**

Fun Fact: The *Tyrannosaurus* was one of the largest meat eaters of all time. At 20 feet high, more than 40 feet long, and weighing more than 7 tons, the *Tyrannosaurus* would be too large to fit on a school bus. Would you ride on a *Tyrannosaurus's* back?

When playing kickball at recess and running along, do your friends wish your toenails were not quite as long?

When you smile, does everyone nearby shriek at the size of your pearly-white, razor-sharp teeth? Some signs are really hard to ignore. It surely sounds like you're a dinosaur!

**Velociraptor
(veh-loss-ih-RAP-tor)**

Fun Fact: Did you know the *Velociraptor* had very sharp claws on both its hands and feet? Playing kickball would be really difficult for them. They also had a mouth full of close to 60 very sharp teeth. Would you shriek if a *Velociraptor* smiled at you?

When walking home from school, does the earth start to quake? Do the nearby buildings start to shake?

Do you have a really large appetite? Can you eat all the food in the refrigerator in just one bite?

Anyone else's tummy would be very sore, but ask yourself this: would a dinosaur's?

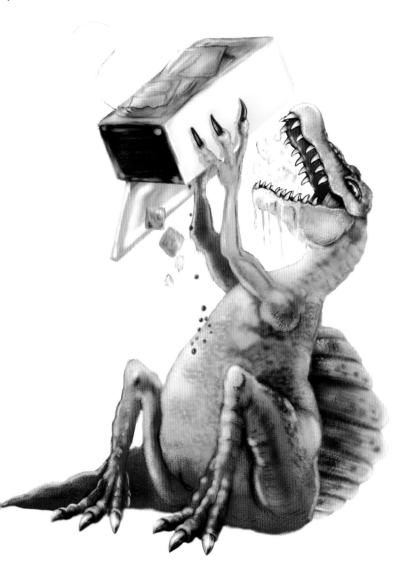

When doing math homework, do you always use your head? Do you count your fingers and toes, or do you count your horns instead?

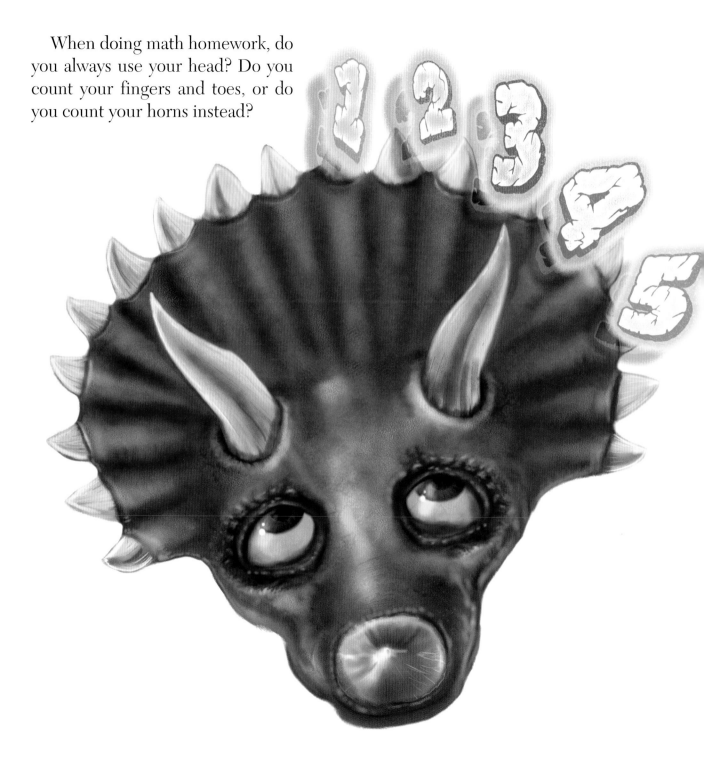

Can you fit in your bathtub, or is it just too tight?
Do you have to take your bath in a lake each night?
Then you don't have a sickness and you don't need a
cure. You may just be a dinosaur!

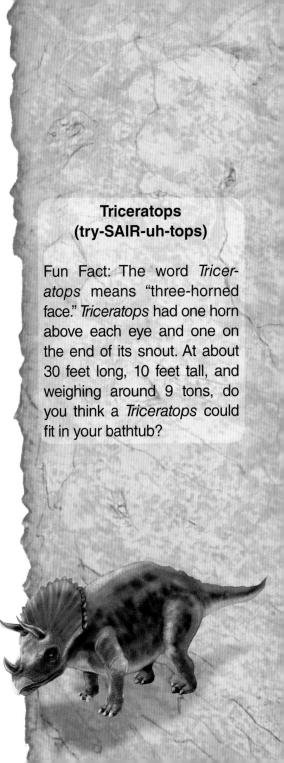

**Triceratops
(try-SAIR-uh-tops)**

Fun Fact: The word *Triceratops* means "three-horned face." *Triceratops* had one horn above each eye and one on the end of its snout. At about 30 feet long, 10 feet tall, and weighing around 9 tons, do you think a *Triceratops* could fit in your bathtub?

When you are tired after a long, long day, would
you rather sleep in a bed, the grass, or a cave?

When you close your eyes, what do you see? Do you count gliding dinosaurs instead of jumping sheep to fall asleep? Then I've said it before and must say it once more. You may just be a dinosaur!

Now don't get me wrong, you may just be a kid who's about as tall as a tree, who has a long tail and razor-sharp teeth, with plates down your back, horns on your head, who can eat a fridgeful of food, and who roars when you speak.

This could very well be but is unlikely and, therefore, you may just be a dinosaur!

Microraptor (MY-cro-RAP-tor):

Fun Facts: *Microraptor* was one of the smallest dinosaurs found. It was the size of a pigeon and had four wings, one on each of its legs and arms—perfect for gliding from tree to tree. Do you think dinosaurs would have counted gliding *Microraptors* if they had a difficult time sleeping?

Scientists can't know for sure how dinosaurs slept, but they believe that dinosaurs with two legs laid down to sleep while four-legged dinosaurs slept standing up. Would you have a hard time sleeping while standing up?

Bibliography

Castro, Joseph. "Spinosaurus: The Largest Carnivorous Dinosaur." *Live Science*. Last modified October 30, 2014. Accessed February 5, 2015. http://www.livescience.com/24184-stegosaurus-facts.html.

Cox, Barry, R. J. G. Savage, Brian Gardiner, and Colin Harrison. *The Illustrated Encyclopedia of Dinosaurs & Prehistoric Creatures*. New York City: Cartwell Books, 2011. 121, 131, 166-67.

Zimmerman, Kim. "Stegosaurus: Bony Plates & Tiny Brain." *Live Science*. Last modified October 22, 2012. Accessed June 27, 2014. http://www.livescience.com/24184-stegosaurus-facts.html.

"Velociraptor facts." BBC Walking with Dinosaurs. Accessed June 27, 2014. http://www.walkingwithdinosaurs.com/dinosaurs/detail/velociraptor/.

Holtz, Jr., Thomas. *Dinosaurs: The Most Complete, Up-to-Date Encyclopedia for Dinosaur Lovers of All Ages*. New York City: Random House Children's Books, 2007. 94-97.

Welsh, Jennifer. "Tiny Four-Winged Black Dinosaur Sported Shimmery Black Feathers." *Live Science*. Last modified March 8, 2012. Accessed June 27, 2014. http://www.livescience.com/18934-dinosaur-black-iridescent-feathers.html.

"Microraptor." BBC Nature. Accessed June 27, 2014. http://www.bbc.co.uk/nature/life/Microraptor

"How did big dinosaurs like the T. rex and argentinosaurus sleep?" BBC Walking with Dinosaurs. Last modified January 17, 2012. Accessed June 27, 2014. http://www.walkingwithdinosaurs.com/news/post/how-did-big-dinosaurs-like-t-rex-and-argenti/.

Hill, Karen. "How Did Dinosaurs Sleep and Did Prehistoric Dinosaurs Sleep Standing Up or Lying Down?" Big Site of Amazing Facts. Last modified July 7, 2010. Accessed June 27, 2014. www.bigsiteofamazingfacts.com.